When Mama Goes to Work

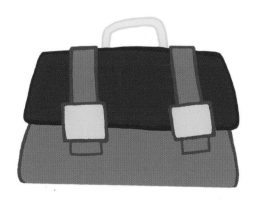

Published in Canada by Fitzhenry & Whiteside, 195 Allstate Parkway, Markham, Ontario L3R 4T8
Published in the United States in 2013 by Fitzhenry & Whiteside, 311 Washington Street, Brighton, Massachusetts 02135

www.fitzhenry.ca   godwit@fitzhenry.ca

10 9 8 7 6 5 4 3 2 1

Library and Archives Canada Cataloguing in Publication
Skrypuch, Marsha Forchuk, 1954-, author
        When Mama goes to work / Marsha Forchuk Skrypuch ; illustrated
by Jessica Phillips.
ISBN 978-1-55455-314-3 (bound)
        I. Phillips, Jessica, illustrator II. Title.
PS8587.K79W44 2013   jC813'.54   C2013-904809-X

Publisher Cataloging-in-Publication Data (U.S.)
Skrypuch, Marsha Forchuk.
        When mama goes to work / Marsha Forchuk Skrypuch ; illustrations by Jessica Phillips.
[32] p. : col. ill. ; cm.
Summary: Through the lives of several children and their working mothers, this book shows how families keep each other in their thoughts even when they're far apart.
ISBN: 978-1-55455-314-3
1. Mother and child – Fiction – Juvenile literature. 2. Working mothers – Fiction – Juvenile literature. I. Phillips, Jessica. II. Title.
[E] dc23   PZ7.S569Wh 2013

Fitzhenry & Whiteside acknowledges with thanks the Canada Council for the Arts, and the Ontario Arts Council for their support of our publishing program. We acknowledge the financial support of the Government of Canada through the Canada Book Fund (CBF) for our publishing activities.

Cover and interior design by Daniel Choi
Cover image by Jessica Phillips
Printed in China by Sheck Wah Tong Printing Press Ltd.

When Mama Goes to Work

Marsha Forchuk Skrypuch

illustrated by

Jessica Phillips

Fitzhenry & Whiteside

To Mom, Gramma and Baba,
for leading the way.

—Marsha

For Mom.

—Jessica

When Mama goes to work,
she wears her working clothes.
She packs my lunch.
She combs her hair.
She takes her special bag.

When Mama goes to work,
I wear my playing clothes.
I pack a lunch.
I comb my hair.
I take my special bag.

When Mama goes to work,
she's busy all day long.
She works with tools
and gets things done.

Mama smiles.

When Mama goes to work,
I'm busy all day long.
I work with tools
and get things done.

I smile.

When Mama goes to work,
she opens up her lunch.
She sees the surprise
that I packed for her,
and it makes her smile.

When Mama goes to work,
I open up my lunch.
I see the surprise
that she packed for me,
and it makes me smile.

When Mama goes to work,
I know she misses me.

But she talks with friends
and thinks of me.
She knows that she'll be back.

When Mama goes to work,
she knows I miss her, too.
But I talk with friends
and we have fun.
I know that she'll be back.

When my day is done,
Mama comes to where I am.
We go to shops.
We sing out loud.
We talk about our day.

When Mama's day is done,
I help her with the door.
We change our clothes.
We cook and eat.
We read a book or two.

When we are at home,
we make a happy mess.
We share a snack,
a goodnight kiss,
and then it's time for bed.

I dream of when I'm big,

and I will work with tools.

I am busy all day long.

Just like Mama...